John Gibson

Reminiscences of Sir Walter Scott

John Gibson

Reminiscences of Sir Walter Scott

ISBN/EAN: 9783337389192

Printed in Europe, USA, Canada, Australia, Japan

Cover: Foto ©Andreas Hilbeck / pixelio.de

More available books at **www.hansebooks.com**

REMINISCENCES

OF

SIR WALTER SCOTT

BY

JOHN GIBSON

WRITER TO THE SIGNET

EDINBURGH
ADAM AND CHARLES BLACK
1871

REMINISCENCES.

Observing from the newspapers that it is intended to celebrate in some way or other the Centenary of the birth of Sir Walter Scott, it occurs to me that this is a fitting occasion for giving to the public some of my own reminiscences of this illustrious man, and a few, out of very many in my possession, of his letters which have not hitherto been printed. Mr. Lockhart's admirable life is so comprehensive and complete, that I believe very little more can be said of much general interest ; but as I am now the only survivor of those who were intimately connected with Sir Walter's affairs during the last ten or twelve years of his life, and as I had more opportunities than any other person of observing the noble exertions he made for the benefit of those whom he had unwittingly involved in his misfortunes, I can, on these matters, speak with some authority, and I wish to say something

bearing rather on his moral worth than on his
intellect and genius, before I also am called
away, which cannot be a distant event.   Should
it be thought that, after all, what I narrate in
these desultory notes is of small consequence, I
can only plead that even trifles connected with
the history of our modern Shakespeare cannot be
altogether uninteresting.

My acquaintance with Sir Walter Scott com-
menced in the year 1822, though I had occasion-
ally met him previously.   At that time, owing to
the infirm health of my friend and old master,
Mr. Hay Donaldson, Writer to the Signet, the
principal charge of his business devolved upon
me, having then myself been a Writer to the
Signet of three years' standing.   Mr. Donaldson
was one of Sir Walter's intimate friends, and
enjoyed much of his confidence in most matters,
though I doubt if he was ever made aware of Sir
Walter's unfortunate connection with mercantile
business, as being actually a partner in the house of
James Ballantyne and Company, printers.   At least
he never mentioned it to me, and at Mr. Donaldson's death, in 1822, when I became Sir Walter's
law-agent, and necessarily enjoyed a good deal of
his confidence, the fact of his being so involved in
business was unknown to me till the catastrophe

in January 1826, when concealment was no longer possible.

Mr. Donaldson was well acquainted with Sir Walter's mother, a sister of Dr. Daniel Rutherfurd, Professor of Botany in the University of Edinburgh, a lady of much intelligence, and to whom, I suppose, her son was indebted for his own mental superiority, in so far as genius and talent can be considered hereditary. Mr. Donaldson repeatedly mentioned to me circumstances connected with Sir Walter's early life which he had learned from his mother, and one of which occurs to me as so singular as to be worth repeating. When a young child, his nurse took him to Arthur's Seat, and under a maniacal impulse took with her a pair of scissors, with the intention of cutting the child's throat. Providentially her courage failed her, but when she returned she told what she had intended to do, and showed the scissors she had taken with her. It need not be added that care was taken she should never have another such opportunity.*

In reference to Sir Walter's lameness, his mother, after he became eminent, used to speak

* It did not occur to me till very lately, that this incident is referred to by Sir Walter Scott in his autobiography. He, however, makes the scene not Arthur Seat, but the crags at Smailholm ; and, of course, his must be the correct account.

of his infirmity as a *blessing,* adding, that but for it he would have been a soldier, and would in all probability have fallen in battle.

On the death of Mr. Donaldson I received a very kind letter from Sir Walter, continuing his law business under my charge, and adding, " I expect Major ——— in eight or ten days. Perhaps you would not think it too much trouble to begin our personal acquaintance by a visit to this place when that gentleman comes here, and we can then better settle what is to be done in the matter.

" I begin to think that I cannot do better than pursue a sale of my teinds next Session, for grain will scarce ever, if produced at all, be cheaper than this year.—I am, dear Sir, your obedient servant,   WALTER SCOTT.

"ABBOTSFORD, 12*th October* 1822."

In consequence of the invitation in the above letter, I paid my first visit to Abbotsford in the early part of November 1822. When I arrived Sir Walter was out of doors, walking in his woods, and I was put into his business room, where I found his table covered with books, some of which I saw referred to the Isle of Man. From this it was natural to conjecture that the next tale would

refer to that island, and accordingly the next was
" Peveril of the Peak." It is needless to say that
this visit to me was most interesting, and Sir
Walter's manner very kind. Several friends were
residing in the house, all of whom, with Sir
Walter's own family, have now, alas ! passed away.
Mrs. Lockhart sung such old ballads as her father
wished, accompanying them on the harp, and a
gentleman, with great spirit, and to Sir Walter's
great gratification, sung, " Blue bonnets over the
Border." The whole evening passed off pleasantly,
but quietly, as befitting a domestic party, the conversation being every now and then enlivened by
one of Sir Walter's innumerable stories.

I had not at this time been distinctly informed
that Sir Walter was the author of all the Waverley
Novels, but, like most people not in the secret, was
always satisfied with the argument, who else could
it be ? When " Peveril of the Peak " appeared,
a copy was handed into my house with the words,
" From the Author " on the fly-leaf, but not in
Sir Walter's own handwriting ; and in like manner a copy of every succeeding work was sent me
with the same inscription. This, of course, would
have settled the question with me, even if I had
previously had any doubt, which I had not. So
long as the authorship was not expressly avowed,

I felt a delicacy in thanking Sir Walter for his
kindness, but after it became necessary to state
the authorship publicly, I took an opportunity of
thanking him, when he told me that it had always
been his custom to give his publisher a list of the
parties to whom he wished copies sent, and added,
"The list was always headed by our Royal Master."

In reference to the supposed authorship of the
novels before it was made public, it was often remarked as a proof that they were all Sir Walter's,
that he was never known to refer to them, though
they were the constant topic of conversation in
every company at the time.   I recollect, however,
one striking instance to the contrary.   In the
month of January 1821, a dinner was given in
the Waterloo Rooms, Edinburgh, to a large party
of gentlemen—I think about forty—to celebrate
the serving Heir, as it is called in Scotland, of a
young gentleman to the large estates of his ances-
tors.   Sir Walter having been Chancellor of the
Inquest, also presided at the dinner, and after
the usual toasts on such occasions, he rose, and,
with a smiling face, spoke to the following effect:
—"Gentlemen—I daresay you have all read of a
. man called Dandie Dinmont, and his dogs.   He
had old Pepper and old Mustard, and young
Pepper and young Mustard, and little Pepper and

little Mustard ; but he used to say that 'beast or body, education should aye be minded ; a dog is good for nothing till it has been weel entered ; I have always had my dogs weel entered.' Now, gentlemen, I am sure ———— has been weel entered, and if you please, we shall drink to the health of his guardians."

The toast was received with the usual demonstrations of applause, and when the noise ceased, an old gentleman—Mr. Williamson, then of Cardrona—addressing the chairman, said, " Sir Walter, you are the best writer of novels we ever had." Sir Walter's reply was of course anything but an admission, and was received with much laughter, but I do not suppose any one who heard him really was deceived. Of all that numerous party, I think there is only one now surviving besides myself.

His denials of authorship were, I believe, rather intended as a reproof to parties asking questions which they had no right to ask, than to convey a false impression. Mr. Lockhart's opinion also, I have no doubt, was correct, that one object of the concealment was " to escape the annoyance of having productions actually known to be his made the daily and hourly topics of discussion in his presence." Probably also, the author thought that the

mystery of the authorship might increase the
public interest in the works. Different opinions
have been expressed as to the propriety of these
denials, which were probably painful to Sir Walter himself ; and, after the success of the first and
second of the novels, one hardly sees the necessity for the concealment at all. The intrinsic
merit of the works was too great to make any
indirect means of keeping up the interest of the
public in them at all necessary, and their popu-
larity, I believe, would just have been as great if
they had borne on the title-page " By Sir Walter
Scott," as " By the Author of Waverley."

That Sir Walter in private life was most
scrupulously truthful, was well known to all his
friends, and the homage he paid to strict veracity
under the most trying circumstances, was well
shown in his interesting tale of " The Heart of
Midlothian," and his delineation of the character
of " Jeanie Deans," to my mind the highest
female character he ever delineated, not even
excepting the heroic " Rebecca."

I have already referred to Sir Walter's unfortunate connection with a business firm. It would
not be becoming, now that all the parties in-
terested are no more, to revive old and painful
questions which were agitated at one time on this

subject. Certainly nothing could have been more unfortunate than his connection with business ; and Sir Walter's friends would have acted a kindly part had they dissuaded him from embarking in any such undertaking. The result is well known. As a partner of James Ballantyne and Company, Sir Walter of course became responsible for every bill or other document on which the company's firm appeared, and as a system of accommodation bills betwixt the two houses of Archibald Constable and Company and James Ballantyne and Company had been carried on to a great extent, it was found, when the affairs were looked into, and both houses became bankrupt, that the ranking on Sir Walter's estate exceeded £120,000, while, so far as I could ever discover, Sir Walter's own debts, including a fair share of the legitimate obligations of the firm, did not exceed £30,000. At the same time, I do not doubt that the sums paid to Sir Walter in anticipation of works not written were raised by means of the accommodation bills in question. He needed money to carry on his improvements at Abbotsford, and to meet domestic expenses there, which were really forced upon him from his celebrity, as this was supposed to lay upon him the necessity of maintaining an establishment disproportioned to his private fortune, and to

entertain strangers not according to his own rank
and fortune, but according to theirs.   Visitors at
Abbotsford were sometimes also so numerous that
they could hardly be accommodated as Sir Walter would have wished.   Miss Hedley, daughter
of the Reverend Anthony Hedley, incumbent of
Hexham—like Sir Walter, a zealous antiquary—
told me that on one occasion her father was a
guest at Abbotsford, and Sir Walter, when show-
ing him to his bedroom, which was in a part of
the house too near the offices, jocularly remarked,
" In the days of yore we would not have allowed
a Northumbrian Borderer to lodge *so near the
horses*," a characteristic way of apologising for the
vicinity of the stables.

To meet all these sources of expense, it was
very convenient at the time, though ultimately
very disastrous, that money could so easily be
raised by accommodation bills ; and it is certain
that had not Sir Walter been personally liable
for the obligations of Ballantyne and Company,
the banks would not have continued the accommodation to the extent they did.   I was told by
Mr. James Ballantyne himself, that when the
banking-house of Sir William Forbes and Company hesitated to continue their accommodation,
he was obliged to state to them that Sir Walter
was a partner under a regular deed of copartnery,
and this satisfied them.

In the month of January 1826, Sir Walter called upon me at my place of business, and explained how matters stood with the two houses referred to, adding that he himself was a partner in one of them—that bills were falling due and dishonoured—and that some immediate arrangement was indispensably necessary. In such circumstances only two modes of proceeding could be thought of—either that he should avail himself of the Bankrupt Act, and allow his estate to be sequestrated, or that he should execute a trust-conveyance for behoof of his creditors. The latter course was preferred for various reasons, but chiefly out of regard to his own feelings. He was determined, he said, if his life was spared, that no man should lose by him. He knew his powers, and how profitable his works could be made, provided always his creditors gave him the proper indulgence, adding, as I often heard him say afterwards, *" Time and I against any two."* This was his favourite phrase when apprehensions were expressed that he was undertaking more than even he could accomplish. At last, as is well known, he sunk under the effort, but not till he fully accomplished the task he had undertaken. All his household debts were paid in full at once, and meeting with much sympathy from his creditors—at least, with very few exceptions—

he continued to labour until all the creditors of the house of Ballantyne and Company, as well as his own private creditors, received large dividends during his life, and at his death received payment in full, from the proceeds of some policies of insurance on his life, the premiums on which he had regularly paid, and from the sale of some of his copyrights. It is true that such of us as had nothing but his own private obligation received only eighteen shillings per pound, but that was because the creditors had presented him with his library, furniture, and other articles at Abbotsford; which were reckoned to be worth £12,000, equal to a dividend of two shillings per pound on £120,000. This being a voluntary surrender or donation, we had no right to consider it as a deduction from our dividend, so that we also may be said really to have received payment in full. Those creditors who ranked on Messrs. A. Constable and Company's estate, as well as on Messrs. Ballantyne and Company's, and on a London firm involved in these bill transactions, not only received payment of the capital sums of their debts in full, but also received a considerable sum of interest. I make no observations on these facts. I leave the facts to speak for themselves.

As soon as Sir Walter determined to execute a

trust, he proposed that I should be sole trustee, but this, for various reasons, I declined; consenting, however, to undertake the trusteeship, provided that one or more parties approved of by the banks should be joined with me. At the request of the directors of the Bank of Scotland, and with Sir Walter's consent, I had a meeting with them, and explained that he was the sole author of the *Waverley Novels*—that he intended, if a trust was approved of, to devote his future works, as well as those then in progress, to the benefit of his creditors, *asking no discharge*, but merely indulgence in the meantime, and that it was wished the banks should name some one or more to be joined with me to represent them in the trust. *This was the first occasion on which the authorship was authoritatively announced*, although the more public admission was made by Sir Walter himself at a public dinner during the following year. The proposal of a trust being approved of, all the necessary arrangements were readily gone into. The late Mr. Alexander Monypenny, W.S., was named by the Bank of Scotland, and the late Mr. James Jollie, W.S., by Sir William Forbes and Company, two gentlemen perfectly agreeable to Sir Walter, who remarked, when I informed him of the appointment—" Mr. Jollie I do not know personally, though I know him well by

character, but with Mr. Monypenny I am well
acquainted, and still better with his brother, Lord
Pitmilly, whose lot and mine it has always been
idem sentire de Republicâ."

In the management of this trust everything
went on harmoniously, the chief labour devolving
upon myself, but my co-trustees giving their valuable aid and advice when required, and Sir Walter
astonishing us all from time to time by the pecuniary
result of his exertions. Repeatedly, in conversation with him, I expressed doubts about the
possibility of his accomplishing such a gigantic
task, but his answer generally was, " Time and I
against any two ; " and on one occasion he added
he had no fears of his works finding a ready sale,
" for since poor Byron died, there is no one whose
works the publishers care so much for as my
own." I am not quite sure if he did not say
" care for *but* my own." I rather think he did.

Sir Walter transferred his house in Castle
Street, and all it contained, to the trustees, whose
painful duty it was to sell the house and to dispose
of the furniture by auction. At this time Lady
Scott was in very poor health, and, before the sale
of the furniture, had gone to Abbotsford. At
this time I received the following letter from Sir
Walter, wishing a few articles saved from the sale

One of them a very trifle, but the mention of which showed his fond recollection of his worthy mother :—

"MY DEAR SIR—I received in safety the cheque for £230, agreeably to your letter.

"Lady Scott reached this place less fatigued than I expected. We will be much the better of having Mr. Cowan's [the trustee on Messrs. A. Constable and Company's sequestrated estate] advice in disposing of "Woodstock." It will be all in the printer's hands on Monday, so you may advertise when you like. There will be great impolicy in letting it lie printed and unpublished, for the publishing season flies fast, and copies will get abroad.

"I will write fully to Ballantyne on the subject. There is, by-the-by, a large picture of the Cave of Staffa, hanging in what was my room, which was *given* me by the laird, and therefore I should not like to sell it. Also another trifling thing in the dressing-room, a mahogany thing, which is called a *cat*, with a number of legs, so that turning which way it will it stands upright. It was my mother's, and she used to have the toast set on it before the fire, and is not worth five shillings of any one's money.—Yours very truly,

"W. SCOTT.

"ABBOTSFORD, 24 *March* 1826.

B

"I have written to Ballantyne all that occurs to me about the sale, and sent him title-page and whole work. He will communicate on the subject, of course. I broke open this letter again.

"26 *March* (1826)."

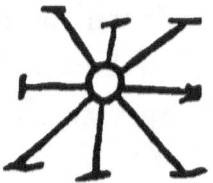

"THIS IS THE CAT."

Of course I secured both the picture and the cat, and sent them to Abbotsford, and I do not envy the man who can laugh at the request for the *cat*. Mr. Lockhart somewhere notices that Scott could never sketch, and the above, which is a facsimile, confirms the remark.

Reference is made in the preceding letter to "Woodstock," which, with the "Life of Napoleon Bonaparte," was in progress at the printing-office when Sir Walter's affairs became embarrassed. "Woodstock" was soon completed, and put at the disposal of the trustees. A London publisher came to Edinburgh in hopes of purchasing the work, and offered largely for the first edition. We soon agreed to terms, but having understood that his credit was doubtful, I refused to enter into any written agreement until he satisfied me that he had the means of paying, or could give a sufficient guarantee for the immediate payment of the price. He anxiously pressed for a settled bargain, and I told him I would meet him in London in a few days, and if he could then satisfy me of his ability, the book was his. I had reason to believe he was on the eve of bankruptcy, as was soon found to be the case. Finding he could not satisfy me, I opened a negotiation with Messrs. Longman and Company, who very readily agreed to the same terms, and paid the money down. Intimating this to Sir Walter from London, I received the following letter in reply:—

"MY DEAR SIR—You have made a glorious sale. Tom Campbell at a literary dinner gave Bonaparte for his toast, alleging for a reason that he had hanged a bookseller. You have overshot one in his own bow, and that is the more difficult task. If we can make anything like the same for Nap., it will let a little daylight in on these matters, and I am sure it will be better worth a corresponding sum.

I should greatly approve of any arrangement which would bring forward the Novels in another

shape.   I think such an arrangement should be
worth £5000 to the funds.

I have nothing to say, but to wish you a good
journey.—Your truly obliged and faithful

"WALTER SCOTT.

"ABBOTSFORD, 14th April 1826."

This result gratified Sir Walter greatly, and I
was told by Mr. Robert Cadell, one of the part-
ners of Archibald Constable and Company (and
who afterwards became Sir Walter's sole publisher, thereby realising a large fortune), that they
were walking together in the garden at Abbotsford when my letter arrived, and, after reading
it, Sir Walter exclaimed, "We shall call this
corner in time coming the Cape of Good Hope."

But he had much trouble after this.   The
creditors of Messrs. A. Constable and Company
claimed the proceeds of "Woodstock," and the
larger proceeds of the "Life of Napoleon Bonaparte," which was published afterwards.   When
these claims were first made, Sir Walter had it
in his power to have suppressed both works, but
he agreed to finish them, under an agreement that
the prices to be received should in the meantime
be consigned in bank, without prejudice to the
claims of either party.   Messrs. A. Constable and

Company's creditors also maintained that Sir Walter was bound to give them two additional Tales, for which they had paid him some money in advance. How they were to get these Tales, not one word of which was written at the time, it was not easy for them to show, but it was very evident that, from the ranking of Constable and Company's creditors on Sir Walter's estate, the advances, whatever they had been, would be much more than compensated. To settle all these questions, a submission or arbitration was entered into betwixt James Ballantyne and Company and Sir Walter Scott on the one part, and the trustee on Archibald Constable and Company's estate on the other, to the Honourable Alexander Irving, Lord Newton, in the month of May 1826; and, after a great deal of discussion, the claim of Messrs. A. Constable and Company's creditors to the proceeds of "Woodstock" and "Napoleon," which were lodged in bank pending the discussion, was repelled. Various other questions were agitated in this submission, but, so far as Sir Walter Scott's affairs were concerned, the above was the most important, and the decision enabled the trustees to pay the first dividend to the creditors.

In the course of the proceedings in the submission, I prepared a statement and argument on behalf of James Ballantyne and Company and Sir Walter, which I intended to have laid before counsel, but, before doing this, I sent it to Sir Walter, on 29th May 1826, for his perusal. He was then living solitarily in a lodging-house, No. 4 North St. David Street, a house now taken down, and on the site of which stand the offices of the Imperial Insurance Company. He had gone to this humble residence when his house in Castle Street came to be sold, and, as Lady Scott was then seriously ill and at Abbotsford, it may be supposed he had no little anxiety on his mind. I think it was about five o'clock in the afternoon when I sent him my memorandum on the points under discussion, and next morning, about ten o'clock, I received the following letter :—

"My dear Sir—I enclose your memorial, which seems very distinct, and I also enclose some notes of my own general views on the subject. I think a bookseller, who can no longer be a *publisher* in the proper sense of the word, has no title to demand a work which he had bargained for expressly in order that he might publish it. You will observe the arguments I have used, which, if you and the other trustees approve, I would submit to counsel.—Yours truly,

"WALTER SCOTT.

"*31st May* 1826."

The notes mentioned in the preceding letter are also referred to in his Diary as follows :— " Wrote this morning a memorial on the claim which Constable's people prefer as to the copyrights of ' Woodstock ' and ' Napoleon.' " (See Lockhart's " Life," first edition, vol. vi., p. 397.) Considering the short time occupied, and the circumstances under which it was written, I have always considered that this paper is one of the most remarkable proofs of Sir Walter's indefatigable industry and power of rapid composition. It is probably too long for such a light publication as this, and there are repetitions in it, but I think it better to give it entire than to attempt to abridge it, and I may add the manuscript is beautifully written, with hardly a single word altered. It is as follows :—

" A general question of the greatest importance occurs, entirely separated from the particular position of certain works, and which so decidedly embraces most of the cases before the arbiter, that, if decided in favour of Sir Walter Scott, it may render the consideration of specialties altogether unnecessary. It involves the nature of the obligation incurred by a bookseller who agrees with an author to publish one or more editions of a work, and the effect which the bankruptcy of such a bookseller must have upon the transaction, supposing the work still in the hands of the author.

"It must be presumed that in this case the bookseller does not buy the property of the book itself,—nay, he does not buy in a proper sense the property of the very edition to which the bargain refers. He buys only the right of publication, and in buying it becomes obliged to publish accordingly. He cannot, against the author's consent, make a bonfire of the books; he cannot even lock them up in his warehouse, and say that the author may keep the copy-money and he will keep the copies. By doing so the greatest prejudice might be sustained by the author, whose literary character would be thus injured, and his means of coming before the public intercepted by the very person who had become bound to produce his works to the world. Were the bookseller to see any good reason, from the tendency of the work or otherwise, to decline publication, he could only do so by placing the printed edition at the author's disposal, and abiding the chance of damages for breach of contract.

"The profession of a publisher being, as the word implies, the publication of books, it is submitted to counsel, as a question of deep import, whether, if before a work is completed, and while it is still in the author's hands, or perhaps in his brain, the publisher should give up his profession or become insolvent and incapable of carrying it on, the author shall be nevertheless obliged to fulfil his part of the bargain.

" Upon the side of the bookseller we may easily conceive circumstances which might void the treaty betwixt him and the author. Suppose the author were to be afflicted with idiocy or lunacy during the printing of a work, it cannot be supposed that the bookseller who has contracted to purchase and publish common sense at least, should be compelled to give value for and produce to the world the ravings of insanity or dotage or idiocy. Or suppose the author dies, can it be supposed that the bookseller is obliged to accept the services of his heir or his executor to complete a work which was left in progress? Surely this will not be alleged. When fulfilment of a contract has become impossible by the death or disability of either party, it is dissolved of course, and the arrangement of such loss as may arise to either party must be arranged *secundum bonum et æquum*,—the publisher restoring the unfinished work, and being of course reimbursed of the expenses incurred, while the friends of the deceased must take their own measures respecting the publication as they shall think advisable.

Such cases occur every day in the trade, as it is called, though they do not get into Court, because there are obvious motives on both sides which lead to extra-judicial arrangement.

"It is therefore clear that if the author becomes incapable of continuing the work, the bookseller is not under the necessity of accepting any substitution of labour, the contract is voided by the incapacity of one of the parties to discharge his share of it. From the parity of reasoning proper to a *bonâ fide* contract, it would seem that if the bookseller becomes incapable of performing his part of the contract by *publishing* the work, and that in his own name, and with the advantages to be expected from the rank he held in the trade at the time of making the contract, the author cannot in reason be held bound where the bookseller would have been free.

"It has been assumed as an undoubted principle that the bookseller is obliged to *publish*—to place the book on his counter, advertise it to the public, subscribe it among the trade, and, in short, go through the ordinary forms. He is not entitled to suppress it. The author has a valuable interest in his works being given to the world, not merely on account of his literary reputation, but because, when the edition which he has sold to the bookseller is disposed of to the public, he has a right to sell others on his own account. This reversionary right, which, in several instances that have occurred between the parties in this case, has been found worth several thousand pounds, would be entirely defeated were the publisher entitled to withhold the first edition from the public. Nay, the case is not much dissimilar even when the bookseller has acquired the whole copyright, for although the author may have no reversionary interest in this especial work, yet his interest with the public must rise or fall according to its success ; and a bookseller, by keeping up an author's first work, might effectually prevent him from finding means to dispose of another. From this doctrine, which seems indisputable, it seems to follow not only that if the bookseller refuses to publish the work, but that if he becomes *incapable* of publishing it, the same consequences must follow as if the author were to become incapable of writing it. If, therefore, the bookseller has resigned his business, or is deprived of the management, or has left the country,—is, in short, incapable of performing his part of the contract by being *bonâ fide* the publisher of the work, the author, on accompting to him for expenses incurred, has surely the same right of resiling which the bookseller would have possessed had the incapacity been on the side of the author.

"It may be thought at first sight that this difficulty may be solved by the bookseller transferring all the duty of publishing, with the incumbrances on the one hand and the profits on the other, to some other person of the trade. But to sanction this transaction against the author's will, or even without his concurrence, would be to strike the deepest blow at literature, by depriving the author of the choice of a publisher, an option most vitally important to his interest and to his character, so much so that any author of common sense or feeling would rather renounce the emoluments of his work than form an unworthy connection of this kind.

"In no profession under heaven are there so many and such singular shades of gradation as among booksellers, or, as they are more properly called, publishers, and the question with respect to selecting a publisher is one of the most important which can occur to a man of letters in the course of his career. The circumstances tending to influence such a choice are as various as important. There are men in the trade the respectability of whose names would accredit works of a very dubious tendency, and there are such as would discredit the 'Whole Duty of Man.' There are publishers whose imprint would sell to a certain extent the most paltry catchpenny that

ever came from Grub Street, and there are others
upon whose shelves and counters the most popular work would become stationary. The connection of the booksellers with the works of periodi-
cal criticism will affect a work bearing their imprint, favourably or otherwise. Their place of
residence is a consideration not to be despised.
The branches of learning in which they have particularly dealt may recommend them or otherwise. In short, not even in the amount of his
copy-money has an author such a deep interest
as in the choice of the person on whose exertions
as a publisher the success of his labours must in
a great measure depend. His choice, therefore,
rests on a distinct *dilectus personœ*, and therefore must be construed as attaching personally to
the publisher agreed upon a faculty which he is
to exercise in person, and which he cannot in
justice be permitted to indorse away to another.

"Would it, for example, be tolerated that any
respectable bookseller, aware that he was under
an obligation to publish a work, should endeavour
to evade a distinct obligation simply by saying,
'I have changed my mind ; I will not put my
name on that imprint ; but here is Mr. ————,
who is quite willing to do so.' The answer is
obvious. The author has the same right to the
publisher's name which in many instances the

publisher has to his, and may positively refuse
such a transference, either upon grounds alleged,
or simply because he is entitled to call on his
contracting party to stand to his bargain.

" If the bookseller has no right to compel de-
livery of a manuscript unless he is able and willing to act as a publisher, it does not appear by what
means Messrs. Constable and Company's creditors
can acquire a right which was not in Messrs. Constable themselves. To the great risque and patrimo-
nial loss of Sir Walter Scott, amongst others, this
great house, who conducted business on a most
liberal plan, and had the means of pushing their
sales to an extraordinary extent, have been obliged to give up business, and counsel are therefore requested to consider whether, having ceased
to be publishers, they can, after the *cessio fori*,
which is compared to civil death, claim the exe-
cution of a *bona fide* contract on the side of the
author, which, unfortunately, their own circumstances prevent them from implementing upon
theirs. It is obviously a very different thing to
deal with a solvent house and with their trustee,
and supposing the copy-money to be paid, the
author cannot be compelled to intrust his work
with them whose situation exempts them from
every species of legal process should any question
of right come between him and them; and he

objects still more that Messrs. Constable and Company, having it no longer in their power to give him the advantage of their own extensive connections, skill, and experience in managing their works, should draw an advantage by turning them over to any one they please, while the author, to whom (however inevitable) they are in fact breaking their contract, is subjected both to the loss of their services and of the extra price which he might have obtained from some other booksellers in compensation of this disappointment.

" If the transaction had been concluded by the works having passed into Mr. Constable's warehouse, the author must have satisfied himself in this as in other cases. But he contends he is entitled to retention on the productions of his own imagination. He knows no species of coercion by which he could be compelled to write, and still less any by which he could be compelled to write against his *will*, without which Messrs. Constable's creditors would be very little benefited by his labours. It is submitted to counsel that the author has the strongest possible hypothec upon that which, independent of his own voluntary exertions, can never have an existence, and that the circumstances which call upon him to exercise such a hypothec for himself and others are very imperious.

"The author transacted business with Messrs. Constable and Company with the utmost confidence and liberality, and it must be supposed that he was well aware that, by carrying his publications into the market, he might have derived higher emolument. But he preferred transacting business with a house whom he knew to be very active and liberal in their dealings with the trade (a thing advantageous to his interest as an author), and perfectly responsible in point of security. Unhappily, it has proved otherwise, and Messrs. Constable, unable to keep their engagements with the author, have become the means of his disappointing others. The readiest mode of extricating these affairs rests upon the author's own exertions, and the question is whether he is free to use these exertions for his own interest and that of his creditors, or whether he is to be chained to the oar for behoof of Messrs. Constable, through whose misfortunes it is that the labour is become at all a matter of compulsion.

"Two of the bargains are mere matters of inference, and if they shall be found binding, it will be in very singular circumstances, for no price was fixed—no time of publication settled—not an item of any serious stipulation entered into. The booksellers, or their trustee, think it their duty to found upon what they supposed and understood. But, surely, there is one general understanding, if such should be admitted, which must be presumed in favour of the author, namely—he thought he was contracting with persons not obnoxious to such an accident as has taken place, and who were to continue to carry on trade in the same manner which had been previously satisfactory to him. But if Sir Walter Scott is held obliged to part with these works at present, Messrs. Constable cannot publish them in the common and useful purpose of the word, nor do they propose to do so. They only desire a share of the profit, for which share they neither have done nor propose to do anything. In short, look at the case on all sides, it just stands thus:—the author has put many thousand pounds into the pocket of the booksellers. The booksellers, besides standing indebted for large sums of copy-money, have actually borrowed several thousand pounds of the author; and the question now is, whether, while they can make good no engagement whatever towards him, they have any title to quarter themselves upon the profits of his labour.

"Sir Walter Scott does not in the least doubt the inclination of Messrs. Constable and Company to do him every justice, or the propriety of the trustee in bringing a demand which he thinks

C

may be made available.   But the hardship of his
own case, who is about to be made a loser on all
sides, is not the less striking."

" ADDITIONAL NOTE.

" It may perhaps be assumed that a populaɪ
work has not the same need of the publisher's
care and patronage as one by an author altogether
unknown.   But this can make no alteration on
the nature of the contract, nor can there be one
law for popular, another for unpopular authors.
And it would, under favour, be a strange plea to
say that the less occasion which an author had
for the good services of his publishers, the rather
is he obliged to pay for what they can no longer
give, and he perhaps does not particularly want.

" But, besides the assistance which the publisher is expected to give the work in the way of
sale, he is also, in most cases, the depositary of
much confidential communication, reposed in him
in consequence of the author's personal good
opinion of him, and which he surely can have no
warrant to transfer, without the author's will and
against his knowledge, to a third party, unknown
to him, or disapproved of by him.   On this occasion
Messrs. Constable and Company are under solemn
obligation not to mention the name of the author,

but this would be to very little purpose if they are entitled to name their own successor to the duty of publishing a work which is not yet printed, forcing thus a stranger upon the author's confidence, and obliging him to hold the confidential and intimate correspondence (which must subsist while a work passes through the press) with any one who will give his creditors sixpence more for a copy, whatever be the character of the substitute, or the injury done to the author's views and feelings.

" An analogous case would be, that a Mail Coach Company hire a driver for their carriage, and just when it is about to start he breaks his arm or is thrown into jail. Would it occur to any one that the poor man's incapacity to fulfil his own share of the bargain gives him any right to say, 'It is true I cannot drive myself, but here is my friend, an excellent whip, pray let him mount the box, and he is obliging enough to give me a premium for substituting him, and I will have the pleasure of drinking your good health out of the first end of the money.' Would it not be sufficient answer that the Company sustained enough of loss from the real Simon Pure *not* driving, without acquiescing in his deriving a revenue on that account from him who actually *did* drive?

"The booksellers here are seeking to get a gain for which they are to return nothing. They desire to remain riders on an undertaking when they cannot discharge any part of the stipulated duty any more than Prospero could have raised spirits after his wand was broken. On the other hand, the author who has lost the services of his booksellers, is desirous to avoid the heavy loss of paying those as publishers who are no longer such—who can only bring his work to the public by putting it into other hands, and retaining a large share of the profits of the work for being a sort of middleman betwixt the author and the actual purchaser."

———

So far as could be discovered, no similar question had ever been raised in any court of law either in England or Scotland, but Sir Walter's views and arguments were pressed upon Lord Newton, and after some discussion, his lordship repelled the claim of Messrs. A. Constable and Company's creditors to the proceeds both of "Woodstock" and of the "Life of Napoleon Bonaparte," and adjudged them to belong to Sir Walter Scott's trustees. The two works were sold by me as printed books, the expense of paper and printing having been defrayed partly by James Ballantyne and Company, before their insolvency, and partly by the trustees afterwards. The purchasers of the first edition of the work (with the exception of a limited number of copies sold to Mr. Cowan, as trustee for Messrs. A. Constable and Company's creditors) were Messrs. Longman and Company, who behaved very liberally in all their transactions with the trustees. Of "Woodstock," 9850 copies were sold for £9500 ; and of the "Life of Napoleon," 8000 copies were sold for £18,200, and these sums, with some other funds realised, were speedily divided among the creditors. The ultimate copyrights were of course retained, and have been very productive since, as parts of other editions of Sir Walter's works.

It will occur to any one who looks at the above details how speedily Sir Walter could have extricated himself from all his difficulties, if his affairs had not been encumbered with the claims of parties for whom he became responsible, by being a partner in the printing establishment.

On 26th July 1827, he wrote me about the "Chronicles of the Canongate," and other matters, as follows :—

"DEAR SIR—Your very acceptable letter of the 24th reached me yesterday. Your ways and means as there stated appear correct. It would be easy to carry on the " Canongate Chronicles " to two volumes more, so as to make the price agreed on, and part of it payable at Mart^s· I will put other irons in the fire with all despatch, but I must let the folks digest Napoleon, for he is a lump for the stomach of a boa-constrictor.

" Much may be said about the claim of Constable's creditors for the works contracted for. One thing is clear—damages must arise to them in place of actual fulfilment, and these damages will be compensated by the large debt they owe me. Specific implement would be undesirable on all sides, for, if they could compel me to write a romance, they could not, by any process I know of, force me to make it a good one. Indeed, I still can see no good reason why I should not have retention on the work in my hands for debt due by the contracting parties in the right of Ballantyne and Company as well as on my own. Enough of this ! We have turned one sharp corner. We will hope the best for the others.

" Adieu ! my dear sir. I am very grateful to you and your obliging assistants, Mr. Monypenny and Mr. Jollie, for all the assistance your kindness has given me. My own exertions shall not be wanting to make your task easy. We cannot expect to make next year quite so productive as the present. But, with exertion, much may be done.—I am, your obliged and faithful servant,

"WALTER SCOTT.

"ABBOTSFORD, 26 *July* 1827."

I do not think it necessary to detail the disposal of Sir Walter's subsequent works. He went on labouring for his creditors to the last, resolving, as he often said, that if possible no one should lose by him. Referring to a dividend which had recently been paid, he says, in a letter to me of 1st July 1830, " I am in great hopes, under God, at Lammas or Martinmas 1831, to pay a similar sum, which will carry us past the corner."

On two several occasions he did me the kindness to reside two or three days in my house, and I need not say that we felt his visit to be an honour as well as a pleasure. He was anxious not to give trouble ; and one morning, when going out of the house, my wife asked him if he was to dine with us that day, to which he answered in his usual good-humoured way, " Oh, yes, I am coming back to dinner, but just let me go about the house as a tame cat."

I think it was on one of these occasions he told me that, when dining with the Duke of Wellington, and asking his opinion of the comparative merits of the English, Scotch, and Irish soldiers, the Duke said " They were all good, but there might be some difference when the army was short of provisions. In such circumstances, the Guards, who were raised in London, and knew all the London ways, contrived to get what no one else could ; the Scotch, if they got a good dinner one day, had the precaution to keep a part of it for the next, and so did very well ; as for the Irish, having or wanting, they were always ready for fighting : But the regiments raised in the English counties were always best when they had good supplies," or words to that effect.

He was always grateful for any little attention, however trifling. I find the following note to my wife, written after one of his visits, when, of course, she had done what she could to make him comfortable :—

"MY DEAR MRS. GIBSON—I believe my servant has brought away a book of yours, which I return ; and I think I left in the drawing-room two volumes of poetry called *Melange*, or some such foolish name. Will you add to all your

kindness that of looking for and returning them.
—Always your respectful humble servant,

"WALTER SCOTT.

"Tuesday Evening, 6 Shandwick Place."

From his known kindness and supposed influence (which last, by the by, was greatly over-
rated), many parties in distress applied to him to
assist them in their difficulties.   Some of these
he sent on to me, thinking I could be of use to
them in the way of advice.   This became so
common, that on one occasion I recollect he said
jocularly, " You will think I am sending all the
widows in the country to you."

At the commencement of his misfortunes Lady
Scott was in very indifferent health, and died in
the month of May 1826, when his affairs were
still very dark.   On 17th May 1826, immediately
after the death, he wrote me with some direc-
tions, and in his letter adds—" Anne has behaved wonderfully under this severe visitation,
but is, poor thing, much exhausted. She is
gathering strength, however, and if we had Monday over (the day of the funeral) we shall be all
better.

" Letters are sent to Sir Alexander Keith and
his brothers, and to Robert Rutherford, but the

distance is such that they can only be considered as a mark that I remember and value their friendship and consanguinity. I apply the same to yourself.—Yours very sincerely,

"WALTER SCOTT.

" *P.S.*—Opened to say that, if you can procure the assistance of Mr. Ramsay we would prefer him. I liked very much the manner in which he did his duty on another occasion. If the clergyman comes on Saturday and remains till Monday, it will be a comfort."

Mr. Ramsay referred to in the preceding is now the well-known and much respected Dean Ramsay. He was able to go, and went to Abbotsford as wished by Sir Walter.

On one occasion, when in the course of conversation the subject of death was referred to, he remarked, "I am not afraid to die, but I dread the death of the mind before the body : that happened to my father."

Besides the questions as to " Woodstock " and " The Life of Napoleon," various other minor questions had been referred to Lord Newton as arbiter, and as to these his Lordship issued notes of his opinion, which on some points were favourable, and on others unfavourable, to Sir Walter's trustees. In answer to a letter which I wrote him, recommending acquiescence in Lord Newton's views, I received the following :—

" My dear Sir—I am on the whole quite of your opinion that we should not move further in the submission. We must take *bit and buffet.* I only wish for a decision about the manuscripts to get out of disputes at once.

" You will, I know, feel for me when I tell you I have lost, by sudden death, my old and faithful servant Tom Purdie, which has given me much affliction. He was quite well yesterday, and died in the night without a groan or anything that could alarm his family. It is an awful warning.

" Cadell has come from the south with tidings of unabated success in the Waverley works.

" I shall need, I believe, to recal the old factor Mr. Laidlaw, from this loss of Tom Purdie. I fancy the trustees will permit me *in hoc statu* to have the house and field at Kaeside for his occupation. He could do your business on the estate as well as mine, but I cannot well manage these extensive and valuable woods without better assistance than I can have from a writer, and I despair finding another Tom Purdie. There are several months to think of all this.—Always most truly yours,

" WALTER SCOTT.

" ABBOTSFORD, *1st November* 1829."

The manuscripts of most of the novels had been given by Sir Walter to Mr. Constable, on the solemn promise that the authorship should not be divulged, and this promise Sir Walter said had not been kept. On this point, however, Lord Newton's decision was unfavourable, his Lordship holding that the condition of secrecy which had been originally attached to the gift was no longer of any avail. In reference to this, Sir Walter wrote me as follows :—

" I was made acquainted with the arbiter's opinion by Mr. Cowan, who, very politely on his own part, offered me a vote in the mode of disposing of the manuscripts. If they are not mine I do not wish to interfere in the matter in the slightest degree, for though I am clear in equity that Constable had no more right than Burke and Hare had to Daft Tam's body or the remains thereof, I am in no way desirous to protract a business which, I think with you, has been on the whole well settled. So I would close all as well as we can, and am glad this stumbling-block is out of the way. I fancy there is little to prevent a Decree-Arbitral from closing these matters. If the public times allow us, I have little doubt we may make another dividend in two or three years, and perhaps I may be able to make an offer for the liferent of my property if I knew what would be its value.—I am, with great sense of your exertions, always very much yours,

"WALTER SCOTT.

"ABBOTSFORD, 12 *April* 1831."

The manuscripts referred to passed, I think, by purchase into the hands of Mr. Cadell, and are now partly at Abbotsford, and partly in the British Museum. The manuscript of "Waverley" is in the Advocates' Library, and that of the "Bride of Lammermoor" is now the property of my friend Mr. Christopher Douglas, W.S.

Mr. William Laidlaw had been parted with at the commencement of the trust for the sake of economy, and the trustees had appointed a highly respectable writer in the country to manage for them various details connected with Abbotsford, but, of course, he could not give Sir Walter any assistance in managing his woods, which he so dearly loved. Mr. Laidlaw, therefore, was recalled, and remained at Abbotsford till Sir Walter's death, being treated more like a friend than a factor.

But I have no leisure to enlarge these desultory notes, and with very sad recollections I pass to the closing scene of my illustrious friend's

history. All who have read Mr. Lockhart's
work must have felt his description of Sir
Walter's last illness and death as most deeply
interesting. They will remember the dying
man's preference of the New Testament to any
other book, and his requesting Mr. Lockhart to
read to him from the Gospel of St. John.
Ignorant of this at the time, I was anxious to
know how Sir Walter viewed his approaching
change ; and meeting with Mr. Laidlaw soon after
the death, I asked him if he recollected anything
particular that had fallen from Sir Walter on
his deathbed, which I knew he had affectionately
attended. "No," he said, "only I remember
that one fine afternoon, when the sun was shining
bright into his bedroom, but he was very low, I
said, Cheer up, Sir Walter, you used to say, *Time
and I against any two;* upon which he raised
himself on his elbows, pushed back his nightcap,
and merely said, '*Vain boast*'—fell back on his
pillow, and relapsed into silence."

To me these two words spoke volumes. Life's
vain shadows were passing away, and I doubt not
his great soul was then grappling with eternal
realities.

I attended the funeral, but can add nothing to
Mr. Lockhart's account of it. It was a deeply

interesting scene, and the sunless sombre autumnal day on which it took place harmonised well with the melancholy ceremony.

Returning to Abbotsford after the funeral, I joined the very small and quiet dinner-party there, and left next morning. So ended my last visit to Abbotsford. What a contrast to the happy evening of my first visit in November 1822 !

Sic transit !

EDINBURGH, 12 CHARLOTTE STREET,
March 1871.

www.ingramcontent.com/pod-product-compliance
Lightning Source LLC
Chambersburg PA
CBHW030908260626
47169CB00008B/2750

* 9 7 8 3 3 3 7 3 8 9 1 9 2 *